Home Farm Twins

Home Farm Puppies

Titch Plays Tricks

Jenny Oldfield

Illustrated by Kate Aldous

Hodder
Children's
Books

a division of Hodder Headline Limited

A Catalogue record for this book is available from the British Library

ISBN 0 340 79603 0

Typeset by Avon Dataset Ltd, Bidford-on-Avon, Warks

Printed and bound in Great Britain by
The Guernsey Press Co. Ltd, Channel Isles

Hodder Children's Books
a division of Hodder Headline Limited
338 Euston Road
London NW1 3BH

One

'Lay-dees an' gen'lemen!' Helen Moore announced. 'Introducing our very own superstar! He's top of the doggy charts – the cutest, the cleverest, the–'

'Get on with it!' Hannah hissed from behind the barn-door.

Helen glowered in her direction. Then she went on: '. . . the smartest, the most entertaining puppy in the entire world!'

'I can't hold him for much longer!' Hannah warned.

Out in the farmyard, their small audience grew restless. The twins' mum and dad glanced at

1

Jenny Oldfield

their watches while their visitors, Jack and Mandy Steele, coughed and shuffled their feet.

At last Helen got a move on. She made a grand, sweeping gesture towards the barn. 'Here he is, ladies and gentlemen – Trrr-icky Titch the Amaaay-zing Acrobat!'

The black-and-brown puppy heard his name and wriggled free from Hannah's arms. He shot out from behind the door and took a run at the nearest hay bale. *Whoosh!* He leaped and cleared it by a whisker.

'Wow!' Jack Steele was impressed.

His wife, Mandy, clapped as Titch sped on.

Whoosh! The puppy jumped bale number two. *Whoosh – whoosh!* Three and four were easy for him now that he'd gathered speed along the row of bales that the twins had set out.

'Very good!' Mary Moore told Helen and Hannah. 'You've trained him really well.'

Hannah grinned. 'Wait. He hasn't finished yet!'

Titch galloped on, his little legs racing towards the end of the row. *Gallop-gallop-gallop-jump!*

'Whee!' Helen cried. 'Way to go, Titch!'

The puppy cleared the final bale, turned and sped

back to the beginning. He jumped on to the first bale, wagging his stumpy tail.

Hannah ran up to him. 'Sit!' she cried.

Titch sat and looked up at her, his pink tongue lolling, one ear cocked.

'Now beg!' Hannah told him.

He sat up on his hindlegs, letting his soft front paws dangle. His brown eyes were bright, his mouth stretched wide in what looked like a broad grin.

'Aah!' Mandy Steele was completely won over. 'Girls, you've done a brilliant job. That was absolutely wonderful!'

'Down!' Hannah told Titch.

Obediently the puppy hopped down from the hay bale. He trotted jauntily towards the farmhouse door, where his dad, Speckle, sat calmly watching his energetic son perform circus tricks.

'He's amazing, isn't he?' Helen chatted proudly with the Steeles. It was a warm sunny evening in late spring. She and Hannah had spent two days of their holiday training Titch to jump bales. No school, no homework – they didn't have a care in the world.

e agreed. 'I always thought of Titch as
ttle so-and-so,' he said with a grin. 'Of
pups in the litter, he was the one who
fell over his own feet and bumped into things,
wasn't he?'

'Not any more!' Hannah argued happily. She
watched Titch wend his way round her mum and
dad, then squeeze under a wheelbarrow parked near
the trough of geraniums that their mum had been
planting when the Steeles had arrived. He came up
too quickly, banged his head on the barrow and
tipped it on to its side.

'Ouch!' Mandy cried as Titch staggered on towards
Speckle. His legs wobbled and he shook his head.
'He must be seeing stars!'

'Oh no, my plants!' Mary ran to pick up the
scattered geraniums.

'Looks as if I spoke too soon,' Jack admitted.

'Is he OK?' David Moore looked concerned,
until Titch reached Speckle and the big dog
gave the puppy a quick lick, then made him
stand up smartly. Titch's tail soon began to wag
again.

'He's fine.' Helen relaxed. She got back to the

subject she was most interested in. 'We've still got all of our half-term holiday left to teach him more tricks,' she told Jack and Mandy, her eyes sparkling. 'I want to train him to jump over a rail, like ponies do. We're gonna build him a proper jump and paint the rail red and white. It'll look really cool!'

'Titch is a star!' Hannah told the Steeles. Like Helen, she was proud of the silky black-and-brown pup. 'He likes to do these tricks and make us laugh. Even when he falls over or bumps into things, he doesn't seem to mind. He just gets back up and starts again.'

From the step Titch waggled his backside and gave a cheerful yelp. Speckle looked sternly on.

'A little comedian!' Jack laughed.

'He does look like he's smiling,' Mandy murmured.

'I'll give him "smiling"!' the twins' mum grumbled as she went on rescuing her plants.

Helen pulled a secret face. Then, 'Would you like to see Titch jump the bales again?' she said sweetly to the visitors.

Jack looked at his watch. 'Sorry, we don't have time,' he told her, his face growing serious. 'As a matter of fact, though, Titch is the very thing we came to talk to you about!'

'So this little star didn't settle down in his new home?' Jack asked Helen and Hannah over a cup of tea in the kitchen at Home Farm.

After his energetic performance, Titch had snuggled down in his basket close to the stove. He was curled up fast asleep.

Hannah shook her head. 'Fred and Hilda Hunt really did want to keep him at High Hartwell,' she explained. 'And that would've been really good. Titch would've been living on a farm just down the lane and we could've seen him every day!'

'But that was the problem.' Helen took up the story. 'The Hunts live too near Home Farm. Whenever Titch felt like it, he could run out into the lane and scoot up here for a quick visit. And Fred and Hilda are quite old. In the end they said they couldn't keep track of Titch if he was always going to be running away like that. They were scared he would get run over on the road.' She tailed off sadly.

'Hmm, that's a pity.' Jack tapped the table with

his blunt fingers. He fell into deep, serious thought. 'Especially since you did so well to find good homes for the other two littl'uns.'

Hannah sighed. She gazed at the slumbering form, remembering the time not so long ago when there were three puppies in that cosy basket . . .

. . . Toby, Tess and Titch. Speckle was their proud dad and the Steeles' dog, Leila was their mum. The pups had been born at Keld House at the beginning of January. A happy New Year. But then Leila had fallen sick and been unable to take care of the little ones. Jack and Mandy had been busy with lambing on their remote farm, so the Moores had stepped in. In the middle of March the lively trio had come to stay at Home Farm until Leila got better. For Hannah and Helen it had been a dream come true.

'Some dream!' their mum had complained every now and then.

Splosh! Toby had probably just landed in the sink, the water trough, a pond or a lake. The twins would rescue him and towel him dry. The speckled black-and-white puppy would come up fluffy, clean and dry. Mary Moore would shake her head and sigh.

For Toby had always headed straight for water whenever his sharp nose smelled it out. He'd taken the plunge and dragged Speckle, Helen and Hannah into many an adventure before Sally Vincent, the local Doveton vet, had suggested a good permanent home.

'I've been speaking to Malcolm Altham over at Silcott Farm,' she'd told the Moores one Saturday in early May. 'They lost their old dog, Molly, in February and they're on the lookout for a new one. I said I'd mention it to you and the Steeles.'

Malcolm Altham ran a herd of Fresian cows. His farm was surrounded by miles of open fells and it was a long way from Doveton Lake. He was a kind man; tall and quiet with a thoughtful, gentle manner. Toby the adventurer still pulled at the girls' heart-strings but even they had to agree that Silcott Farm was the perfect home . . .

Which left two puppies in the basket – Tess and Titch.

'It's like "Ten in the bed"!' Hannah had sighed.

Helen had nodded. 'They all roll over and one falls out.'

'But that's what we planned,' Mary had reminded

them. 'We told Mandy and Jack that we would take care of the puppies either until Leila was better or until we managed to find nice new homes for them.'

Secretly Hannah and Helen had longed to hold on to Tess and Titch for as long as possible.

'Maybe Mum and Dad won't notice we've still got them!' Hannah had whispered in the privacy of their bedroom.

'Dream on!' Helen had replied.

That had been the day before Tess had gone off to live with Mr and Mrs Hudson at the Shepherd's Dog.

'My wife, Christine, has been nagging me for a little Border collie for ages,' Frank Harrison had told David and the twins when he arrived at Home Farm in his Morris Traveller. 'She reckons it'll be good company for Polly, our Cavalier King Charles spaniel.'

Hannah and Helen had watched glumly as Tess had gone sniffing round the neat little old man's trouser-legs, no doubt picking up Polly's scent. The elderly couple lived in a shiny, old-fashioned pub on Hardstone Pass, about two miles outside Nesfield where Mary Moore ran her café.

'Come and visit us any time you like!' Mr Harrison

had insisted, popping creamy, furry-faced Tess into a snug dog-basket. He'd driven her off in his spick and span old car and both Helen and Hannah had shed a tear.

'Don't worry about Tess,' their dad had comforted them. 'The Harrisons will take care of her. They're real dog people!'

'We're real dog people too!' Hannah had wailed.

. . . Which left only one puppy in the basket.

It was almost the very end of May, coming up to the half-term holidays, when Fred and Hilda Hunt from the farm down the lane had offered to take Titch off their hands.

But whereas Toby and Tess had quickly settled in with their new owners and were said to be perfectly happy, little Titch had turned into a regular runaway.

He'd scarpered up the lane almost as soon as Hilda had taken him down to High Hartwell. Hannah and Helen had been in the barn, gloomily grooming Solo their grey pony and Stevie their stubborn donkey.

' 'S not fair!' Helen had been grumbling out loud, though secretly she knew she didn't have a leg to stand on. After all, the deal had always been to send Leila and Speckle's puppies off to new homes. But now there were no babies left in the basket and Speckle was moping around the house like a poor lost soul.

'What's that noise?' Hannah had heard a scratching outside the door. She'd opened it to see Titch's little face smiling up at her.

'Back to High Hartwell with you!' their dad had insisted as soon as he'd found out.

And again, when Titch had showed up at the kitchen window while the Moores were eating supper. And again, next morning, when Titch stole

across the yard, into the house and was found curled up by the kitchen stove. And again . . .

After two frantic days, Fred and Hilda had admitted defeat.

'Best find him somewhere else to live,' the old farmer had told them. 'It needs to be further afield – a farm on the far side of Nesfield maybe. Then the little rascal won't be able to run back here at every end and turn.'

Helen and Hannah had persuaded their mum and dad to take the last puppy back meanwhile. And so there was one pup back in the basket after all.

'But not for long!' Mary had set up her usual war cry. 'I'll put a notice in the café window, saying we need a good home for an adorable black-and-brown Border collie cross pup. Before you know it, we'll be inundated with offers!'

The twins had blocked their ears – 'La-la-la!' – and set about teaching Titch to jump hay bales.

But now Jack Steele sat down at their kitchen table and put on his serious face. 'Mandy and I have been thinking,' he began. 'Leila is better now—'

'Good news!' David interrupted brightly.

There was a tense pause as Helen and Hannah

guessed what was coming next.

'We're very, very grateful for what you've done for us,' Mandy went on. She tried not to look in the direction of the twins' dismayed faces. 'But the fact is, we honestly feel the time has come to take Titch off your hands!'

Two

'But we're gonna build him a jump!' Hannah stood up from the table, her face aghast.

'Yeah, Titch can't leave until we've taught him to do more tricks!' Helen was equally panic-stricken. The thought of losing the lovable puppy was too much to take. She began to pace up and down, churning out reasons for him to stay. 'You think Leila's better but she might not be. True, she might look well but the strain of having to take care of a lively puppy might make her sick again. Besides, you two must be mega-busy with your lambs . . .'

'Well, yes, we are,' Mandy admitted.

'Right!' Helen cried. 'So you don't have time to train a clumsy pup like Titch!'

'Titch isn't clumsy,' Hannah objected, missing the point completely.

Helen glared. 'All I'm saying is, he's tricky to train, so he takes up more time – get it?'

'Oh yeah – definitely!' Hannah blushed. 'Loads more time.'

Mandy and Jack Steele sighed and glanced at the black-and-brown puppy, still asleep in his basket. 'We hear what you say,' Jack murmured. 'But we don't want the little rascal to outstay his welcome with you good people. As I say, we already owe you a huge favour.'

All this time, the twins' mum and dad had stayed quietly in the background. Helen and Hannah knew full well that there was no point pleading with their parents, they had to concentrate on persuading Jack and Mandy to let Titch stay.

But now Jack was looking directly at Mary. 'You've been patient enough already, waiting for Leila to recover from this kidney complaint. But I'm sure you'll be relieved to have Titch off your hands at last.'

'Not!' Helen and Hannah muttered under their breaths.

Mary smiled and glanced at David. 'We've loved every minute of having the puppies at Home Farm,' she began.

The twins' dad grunted. 'Well, maybe not every minute. We don't mention geraniums, for instance. Or water troughs, or accidents with tractors, or lake rescues, or stampeding sheep, or . . .'

'Uh-hum!' Mary's short cough put a stop to David's list of puppy disasters. 'The fact is Toby, Tess and Titch are three lively little characters and when they're not around, we miss them!'

'We do?' David asked with a bemused look.

'Yes!' Helen and Hannah chimed.

The raised voices woke Titch. He opened his eyes and yawned.

Mary's smile broadened as the puppy stretched, then padded softly towards her. He pounced on the sheepskin trim at the top of her boot, wrestling and growling, then seizing it between his teeth.

'Why not leave Titch here with us while we try to find him a decent home?' she asked the Steeles. 'After all, what difference is another week or so going to make?'

'Did you see Dad's face?' Hannah giggled as she remembered the kitchen scene from the night before. It was early on Saturday morning: she and Helen had taken Speckle and Titch into Doveton village to run errands for their dad.

Helen nodded. 'Did you hear what he said under his breath?'

'Yep. Something like, "Well, blow me down with a feather!" and, "The woman's going soft in her old age! Mutter-mutter!"' Copying their dad's deep voice, Hannah made Helen burst out laughing.

'But he didn't mind really. Dad has a soft spot for Titch, just like the rest of us.' As they reached Luke Martin's shop in Main Street, Helen gave the order for Speckle and Titch to stop outside. The puppy sat down smartly beside his dad, his brown ear cocked, his black ear flopping forward.

'What a little sweetie!' A customer coming out of the shop smiled down at Titch.

Another lady, going in ahead of the twins, stooped down to pat him and say, 'Bless!'

'Stay!' Hannah commanded.

Jaunty little Titch wagged his tail and stayed, good as gold.

'I'll wait outside with Speckle and Titch,' Hannah told Helen. 'Tell Luke to come out and see them.'

So she sat on the bench outside the shop, watching the white doves flutter around Luke's dovecote, a safe distance away from the shopkeeper's smug and superior Siamese cat. Sophie sat on the windowsill, gazing up at the birds with her piercing blue eyes, the tip of her long black tail twitching crossly.

'See, Sophie would really love to pounce on a nice fat dove and have him for breakfast,' Hannah explained the laws of nature to Titch. 'The doves realise that, so they tease her by fluttering out of reach. They fan out their tails and coo away happily, knowing that Sophie is going to stay hungry!'

'*Yeeowww!*' Sophie's weird, flat miaow interrupted the calm scene.

'*Yap-yap-yap!*' Titch replied, running madly at the cat, who stood up, arched her back and spat down at him.

'Oh yeah, that's another thing,' Hannah added, dragging the puppy away from the windowsill. 'Cats don't like dogs chasing them. And cats have very sharp claws, so remember that!'

A subdued Titch sat down again, close to Speckle. Seconds later, Luke came out of the shop with Helen. 'I hear you've been training your puppy to jump hay bales,' he said to Hannah. 'He seems to be turning into a proper little circus act.'

Hannah grinned. 'Would you like to see him sit up and beg?'

The shopkeeper nodded, then pulled a small round dog biscuit from his pocket. 'How about this as a reward?'

Hannah took the biscuit and hid it in her palm. With both hands behind her back, she leaned over Titch and murmured the order to beg.

The puppy tilted his head to one side, nostrils quivering.

'He smells a treat!' Luke grinned.

'*Yeeeowww!*' Sophie cried crossly at the puppy who was stealing all the attention.

'Come on, Titch, beg!' Hannah prompted.

He pricked up his floppy ear, leaned back on his haunches and raised his front paws.

'Good dog!' Hannah beamed, producing the

Titch Plays Tricks

biscuit from behind her back and popping it into Titch's smiley mouth.

'Well done, very impressive!' Luke clapped enthusiastically.

'*Yeeoww!*' Sophie sneered, stalking off out of sight.

'Your little puppy's gorgeous!' Miss Wesley told Helen and Hannah. She greeted them on the lake shore while they were searching for a long, straight piece of driftwood that they could use to build Titch's special jump.

Miss Wesley was their teacher at Doveton Junior and lived at Lakeside Cottage. She was young ('youngish', Helen said), slim ('slimmish', according to Hannah), dark haired and kind ('kindish', said Hannah and Helen, except when you forgot to hand in your homework).

'Titch doesn't belong to us.' Helen told Miss Wesley with a sigh. 'He belongs to the Steeles at Keld House.'

'He does tricks,' Hannah added. 'Would you like to see him jump this long stick?'

The teacher nodded. She watched patiently as

21

Hannah knelt on the smooth grey pebbles to hold the stick at the right height for the puppy to jump. Then Helen took him a few metres along the shore.

'Sit!' Helen ordered.

Titch obeyed, brown eyes gleaming.

'Ready, Hann?'

'Yep!'

Helen bent down and whispered in Titch's ear. 'Go ahead, jump!'

The puppy streaked off along the shore at full gallop. *Whoosh!* He cleared the stick with fifteen centimetres to spare.

'Excellent!' Miss Wesley clapped. But her applause died away when the puppy veered to the left and bounded towards her garden. 'Uh-oh, he's spotted Sinbad!' she gasped.

'Oh no, not another cat!' Hannah could see that Titch had not taken the least bit of notice of her advice outside Luke's shop. *Sharp claws, remember!*

Titch yipped and yapped his way towards the black cat sitting on Miss Wesley's fence. Just like Sophie, Sinbad arched his back and made his fur stand on end. He bared his pointed white teeth and unleashed a venomous hiss.

'Watch out, Titch!' Hannah yelled.

But it was too late. The puppy's stride faltered in the face of the fierce cat. As he stumbled over a big mossy stone, Sinbad pounced. With bared claws and fangs, he landed on top of the tumbling puppy.

'Ouch!' Helen closed her eyes. She'd seen enough.

'*Ssssshhaaah!*' A hissing Sinbad writhed with Titch in a fierce embrace. Then he sprang clear and vanished into the nearby hedge.

'That's one scratched puppy, I'm afraid.' Miss Wesley hurried across with the twins. She watched as Helen picked up a stunned Titch. 'Yes, there's a small cut across his poor nose!'

They saw that the brown fur was marked by a shallow wound which oozed pin-pricks of bright red blood.

'Ouch!' Helen winced again.

Titch lapped up the sympathy and snuggled close.

But Hannah sternly wagged her finger. 'What did I tell you? Cats have very sharp claws, remember!'

'Give it to him straight, Speckle!' Hannah drove home the message as she and Helen returned through the village carrying their piece of driftwood. 'Tell him that cats plus cats equals peace and harmony. Dogs plus dogs ditto. But cats plus dogs equals War with a capital "W"!'

The grown-up dog marched ahead of a sad looking Titch down Main Street. The puppy's nose had stopped bleeding, but the red scratch was still raw.

'Aah, poor little thing!' Valerie Saunders from Doveton Manor pulled up in her Range Rover for a chat with the girls. When she saw Titch's recent battle-scar, she sighed and tutted, then drove on.

'Has he been in the wars?' Luke called from his shop doorway.

After Helen and Hannah had told him the story, he went inside and brought out another biscuit treat. 'Poor little chap,' he murmured, waving them on their way.

In fact, almost everyone they met felt sorry for Titch.

'Ooh, I bet that hurt!' a pregnant Julie Stott commiserated. She was wheeling her son, Joe in his pushchair, heading for her mother-in-law's house which overlooked the village cricket pitch.

Joe reached out a podgy hand to try and pat the puppy. 'Woof-oof!' he cried.

'Yes – little doggy!' Julie told him, careful not to let him touch. 'Joe's moved on from horses,' she told Helen and Hannah. 'Now he loves every blessed thing with four legs!'

They laughed and walked on, bumping next into the only person in the universe who could possibly find fault with their poor wounded puppy.

'Keep that dog on a lead!' a harsh voice called from a garden gate. 'You'll have it running out into the road and causing an accident if you're not careful!'

'Mr Winter!' Helen sucked air through her teeth and cringed.

'D'you two girls hear what I'm saying? You're not fit to have a dog if you don't keep it on a lead!'

Cecil Winter – the grumpiest, meanest, bossiest man in Doveton. And the ex-head-teacher of Doveton Junior School.

'Speckle *is* on a lead,' Hannah replied, holding it up to show the old man. They approached his gate quickly, anxious to get past.

'Not that one. I'm talking about the puppy!' Mr Winter barked gruffly. 'You obviously haven't trained it correctly. It's going to be a real handful when it grows up!'

'Titch is on a lead too,' Helen assured him.

'Harrumph!' The ex-teacher's snort showed that he wasn't ready to back down. Instead, his white moustache bristled and his bushy eyebrows joined together in a deep frown. 'It's been fighting, I see!'

Unluckily Titch had stopped right by the old man's gate and was snuffling by the gatepost. Helen tugged at the lead to make him get a move on.

'Just as I said – it's going to be totally out of control and end up homeless in one of those dreadful dog shelters unless someone who's an expert in training steps in soon!' Mr Winter looked down his nose at Titch, then turned away with a toss of his head. He went up his garden path tutting and grumbling to his heart's content.

'Phew!' Helen drew breath and persuaded Titch to leave the smelly gatepost alone. They walked away double-quick, before the old man could turn back and resume his attack. 'What's eating Cecil today?'

Hannah tried to recall something she'd overheard the vet, Sally Freeman, telling her mum just last week. The memory drifted vaguely into focus as they reached the end of the street and turned up the lane towards Home Farm. Why was Mr Winter in an even worse mood than usual? What could it be?

The question niggled all the way up the hill. Then, 'Got it!' she cried as she, Speckle, Helen and Toby turned into the farmyard. 'I remember now. Sally told Mum that Mr Winter's dog had just died of old age. Apparently he was really upset. In fact, Sally said she was worried about what happen to him now that he doesn't have poor old Puppy to boss about!'

Three

'*Oh, what a beeau-oo-tiful morn-ing,*

Oh, what a beeau-oo-tiful day...' Hannah trilled.

Helen rested the newly painted red-and-white pole on two stacks of flat rocks.

'*I've got a wonder-ful fee-eeling,*

Dah-de-dah dah-dah dee-dah!' she sang.

The sun was shining on the field behind Home Farm. Their dad was walking up the hill with Titch and Speckle at his heels. '*The corn is as high as an el-ee-phant's eye...!*' he boomed in a deep bass voice.

'Shush, Dad, you'll scare the sheep!' Helen giggled

and pointed to John Fox's herd way down in the valley.

He ignored her and went on oompahing. 'That's a smashing new jump you've built,' he commented. 'You see that, Titch? That's specially for you!'

The little pup ran up to the bright striped pole and sniffed. He curled up his black nose.

'Yes, it smells funny,' Hannah admitted. 'That's the paint.'

David crouched beside Titch to examine the pole. He dabbed it gingerly.

'Watch out, Dad!' Hannah cried.

'It's not – quite – dry!' Helen pulled an exasperated face. 'Doh!'

Their dad held up five fingers tipped with red. 'You don't say!' he muttered, then absent-mindedly wiped his hand on his cream woolly jumper.

'Never mind. Let's show Titch what he's supposed to do.' Hannah got on with the business of training the puppy. 'Speckle, you show him!' she invited.

So they all stepped to one side as Speckle trotted easily across the grass, which was dotted with white daisies and pink clover. It smelt sweet and fresh.

Taking up position, Speckle waited for Hannah to give the order.

'Go, Speckle!' she cried.

He sped towards the jump, a low streak of black and white through the flowery meadow. He took off at exactly the right moment and sailed over the jump.

'Hurray!' Helen clapped wildly, then turned to Titch. 'Your turn now,' she told him, trotting him up to the starting position.

'Go, Titch!' Hannah cried from the far side of the jump.

The puppy shot off down the hill, too fast for his little legs to keep control. By the time he reached the jump he was yapping wildly, his ears were flapping and his back legs bouncing him into a disastrous nosedive.

'Uh-oh, no brakes!' the twins' dad groaned.

'Whoops!' Hannah half closed her eyes as Titch's chin hit the ground and he somersaulted into the jump.

Crash! The pole came down on top of him.

With a stunned look, the puppy crawled out from under it.

'Over, not under!' Helen cried, running to join them. She stared at the dizzy youngster, then clamped her hand over her mouth. 'Oops!'

'What? Why?' Hannah opened her eyes. 'Oops!' she echoed.

Titch shook himself then squirmed his head round to sniff at his back. He snuffled and wriggled, rolled over in the grass then sprang on to his feet.

'Red paint!' David was the last to spot the broad splodge of scarlet across Titch's shiny black fur. He made a lunge for Titch and missed. 'Quick, girls, grab him. Let's get back to the farm and find some paintbrush cleaner!' . . . (pounce – miss). 'Helen, I said, grab him, not fall over laughing!' . . . (lunge –

fall flat). 'Hannah, we need a clean cloth to wipe it off. Come on, girls, for goodness sake pull yourselves together!' ... (grab – gather an armful of rolling, wriggling, paint-covered puppy). 'Phew! Quick, let's get the little rascal cleaned up before your mum finds out!'

'There's a good dog!' Hannah cooed at Titch, who stood calmly and patiently on a towel on the kitchen table as she brushed his silky coat until every hair shone.

'Are you sure we got all the paint off?' her dad quizzed.

'Every speck,' Helen assured him. Then she narrowed her eyes. 'Which is more than we can say for some grown-ups around here!'

David looked down at his own hands and jumper. 'Red everywhere!' He admitted that the cleaning process hadn't been without problems. Even his face was smeared scarlet. 'Perhaps I'd better go upstairs and root around in my darkroom,' he muttered. 'May be I'll come across some chemical that has magic cleaning properties!'

So he shuffled off to his workroom and left them

to put the final prettifying touches to Titch's makeover.

'Mum's gonna kill Dad when she sees his jumper!' Hannah whispered, running a steel comb through the ruff of brown fur round the puppy's neck.

'Remind me not to be around when she gets back!' Helen giggled, then turned to a more serious subject than their dad getting killed. 'You know what Mum said about the answer to the advert about Titch?' she asked.

Hannah nodded and frowned. She'd spent the day so far trying not to think about it.

'It's strange!' Mary had said at breakfast time, between bites of toast and rapid slurps of tea. 'I've only had one response to the card in the café window. I would've expected a lot more people to show an interest in adopting a cute puppy like Titch!'

Helen and Hannah had immediately tried to change the subject. 'Can we ride Solo on the fell this afternoon?' Helen had clamoured.

'Please, please, please!' Hannah had added.

'Hmmm? Yes, I suppose so.' Mary had shot them a swift look. 'Don't you want to know about the person who asked me about Titch?'

'No!' they'd chorused.

Their mum had gone ahead anyway. 'She was a customer who was visiting Nesfield with a coach party from Manchester.'

'Manchester!' Hannah had wailed. Manchester was miles away. It was huge. There were no fields and fells in Manchester.

'Yes. She was a member of an over-sixties group. Her name's Dorothy White and she was looking for a puppy to replace a dog who died last Christmas. She said that Titch might be just the one!'

'Over sixty!' Helen had protested. 'But that's ancient. How could she take Titch for walks?'

'Even if there was somewhere in Manchester to walk him!' Hannah had muttered.

Mary had tutted and told them that sixty wasn't ancient and that there were lovely parks in Manchester. 'Anyhow, Dorothy went away saying she would have to think about it. She had to consider her sister, Olive, who lives with her. Apparently Olive would prefer a smaller, quieter breed of dog and Dorothy said she would need about a week to bring her round to the idea of a Border collie cross. But she thought she could probably do it in the end.'

Helen and Hannah had sunk into gloomy silence. Their mum had told them that the pensioner had written down the Moores' phone number and promised to ring in seven days. 'Which takes us to next Thursday,' she'd concluded. 'Meanwhile, I had to warn her that we would still carry on looking for other possible homes for Titch.'

The news had only really sunk in after their mum had left for work, before the girls had found a way to cheer themselves up by building the new jump for Titch. But now that Titch was gleaming again, Helen had remembered the elderly Manchester lady.

'We'll never see Titch ever again!' she whispered sadly.

'Titch will live in a street. There'll only be a tiny garden for him to play in and there'll be loads of fast traffic outside!' Hannah painted a bleak picture of the poor puppy's future.

A new thought struck Helen. 'Unless we find him a better home before Thursday!' she cried.

Her excited voice made Titch yip and jump down from the table. He danced between the girls' feet, wagging his tail, then fighting the corner of the rug by the stove. '*Grr-rrr! Rrrrufff!*'

'A home with lots of space around it!' Helen went on. 'Somewhere we can drop in and visit, like we can with Toby and Tess!'

Hannah nodded. 'Yeah, but we already tried, remember. We sent Titch off to Fred and Hilda's, and look what happened.'

'But the Hunts aren't the only people around Doveton who might want a new dog,' Helen protested. 'And look at how popular Titch is. Everyone thinks he's cute and funny. Remember yesterday when we walked him through the village!'

For the first time since they'd begun to look after the three pups for the Steeles, Hannah really turned her mind to finding one of them a good home. After all, anything was better than Manchester!

Hannah thought back to the day before. 'Yeah, but Luke can't have Titch because of Sophie. Likewise, Miss Wesley. No way would Sinbad put up with having a dog in the house.'

'True,' Helen sighed. 'But what about Dan and Julie Stott?'

Hannah considered the young couple who lived at Clover Farm. They mainly grew wheat but they kept a small herd of pigs as well. 'That'd be good,' she agreed. 'Titch would like it there.'

'Titch would like it where?' their dad interrupted, coming down from the attic. He spied the puppy tunnelling under the rug, just a moving hump under the patterned surface.

'Pooh!' Helen sniffed a sharp whiff of chemicals and frowned at the pink smears down the front of his jumper.

'Titch would like to live at Clover Farm, don't you think?' Hannah said hopefully. 'Dan Stott is really nice and friendly. And he loves his pigs.'

'True enough.' Their dad put his head to one side, reluctant to squash Hannah's hopes yet not wanting her to raise them falsely. 'But remember Julie's about to have her second baby, so I don't imagine they'll want to take on a lively puppy at this point in time.'

'Ah!' Helen and Hannah's faces dropped and their shoulders sagged.

'Who else does that leave?' Helen sighed, as Speckle ran through the open door out into the yard. He barked at a passer-by to let him know that Home Farm was well guarded.

David glanced out of the window at a figure riding slowly uphill on a bike. At first he could only see a fair-haired head and a face red from the effort of the steep climb. But then the boy's full figure came into view. 'Erm, Helen – Hannah!' He beckoned them to the window.

They went and looked out. The boy looked into the yard and stuck out his tongue at Speckle. *Huff-puff-huff*. On he went up the hill.

'Oh no, not that!' Helen groaned. 'Anything but that!'

Huff-puff, up the slope to Crackpot Farm.

'Why, what's wrong with Sam Lawson?' their puzzled dad asked. It was plain that he thought he'd hit on a brilliant idea.

'Everything!' Hannah and Helen cried.

'So you don't think he would be a good owner for Titch?' David insisted.

'No way!' Helen told him.

'Sam's a know-all. His head's this big and we can't stand him, full stop!' Hannah insisted.

Which made their casual Sunday visit to Crackpot Farm very difficult to explain . . .

Four

Helen and Hannah made their way half a mile up a steep hill to reach the Lawsons' farm. Pinkish-white blossom covered trailing brambles at the roadside and pale yellow primroses lined the ditches. Overhead, light wisps of white cloud wafted across a deep blue sky.

'Come here, Titch!' Hannah called as the puppy dived into a ditch. He came up ruffled and gripping a sturdy stick between his jaws.

'No! Bad boy!' Helen had hoped to keep Titch clean and show him off to Sam Lawson at his scrubbed-up best. 'Now look at you!' she wailed.

Titch offered the stick for Hannah to throw. He

41

was covered in tiny blossom petals and caked in mud. Hannah knew she should tell him off as Helen had, but the temptation to play was too much to resist. So she picked up the stick and threw it in a high arc into the nearby field.

''*Owzat!*' A slight figure suddenly sprang up from behind the wall, leaped for the stick and caught it before Titch had even clambered on to the wall.

'Sam!' Helen and Hannah yelled. Their un-favourite neighbour had just ruined the puppy's game.

Poor Titch scrambled over the wall and hunted fruitlessly in the field for his stick.

'Whass-up?' Sam inquired innocently.

'That stick belongs to Titch!' Helen complained, until Hannah dug her in the ribs.

'Better not put Sam in a bad mood,' she hissed. 'Otherwise, he's bound to say no!'

So Helen had to bite her tongue. *Trust Sam Lawson to show off!* she grumbled to herself. *I bet he thinks he should play cricket for England!*

She no sooner thought this than Sam launched the stick into the air for Titch to fetch. It soared twice as high and far as Hannah's effort and landed almost at the edge of Sam's yard. Titch chased the stick, lost sight of it amongst the nettles and was left snuffling along the farmyard wall.

'Dumb dog!' Sam cried scornfully. He stood hands on hips, fair hair ruffled by the wind. 'Can't even find a stick!'

'Titch isn't dumb!' Helen retorted. She dodged before Hannah had time to dig her in the ribs again. 'You just shouldn't throw it so far, that's all!' Scowling, she ran ahead to find the stick for the puppy.

'Anyway, whaddy'a want?' Sam demanded suspiciously, taking a piece of chewing-gum from its silver wrapping and sticking it into his mouth.

'That's t'rrific!' Hannah sulked, walking slowly up the rest of the hill with Sam. The farm stood on the horizon, a solid, low, two-storey building with green gables and window frames. Sam's mum had grown honeysuckle round the porch. 'We come on a friendly Sunday visit and you treat us as if we're foreign spies!'

'You two never come to Crackpot Farm on a friendly visit!' Sam pointed out. 'Unless it's to see Sorrel!'

'Yeah, that's right!' Hannah grabbed the

unexpected lead she'd been offered. 'Helen and me wanted to see the rabbit. How is he – er she – doing?'

'She's OK,' Sam shrugged. 'She should have more babies for me to sell soon. Did you bring her a carrot?'

'No, sorry.' Hannah followed Sam through the gate into the yard, quickly beckoning Helen to follow. 'Spruce Titch up a bit,' she whispered, 'while I keep Sam busy chatting about Sorrel. We've got to make sure that Titch looks good and is on his best behaviour!'

'I never wanted to do this in the first place,' Helen reminded her in an undertone. 'It was your idea to bring Titch to Crackpot Farm.'

'Actually, it was Dad's.' Hannah stopped by the gate to carry on the whispered squabble.

'Yeah well, stupid idea!' Helen scowled at Sam Lawson who was carefully opening the door to the rabbit hutch which was tucked away inside the porch. It seemed to her that his head had grown two sizes bigger since she'd last seen him in school the week before.

'So you want Titch to get sent off to Dorothy and Olive in Manchester, do you?' This was the bottom line, Hannah reminded her – Sam Lawson and Crackpot Farm or the spinster sisters in the distant, gloomy city.

Helen's scowl deepened. 'OK, OK, I'll clean Titch up!' she agreed grudgingly.

'D'you wanna see Sorrel or not?' Sam called to Hannah, lifting a fat black rabbit out of the hutch. 'Cos if you do, you'd better hurry up!'

'What's the big rush?' Hannah asked, approaching quickly. The rabbit blinked at her from the safety of Sam's arms. She was a round, furry ball with long pink ears and black whiskers.

Sam answered impatiently, as if Hannah should be a mind-reader and know what was going on inside his head. 'I'm taking her into the barn for her dinner, where her indoor hutch is. C'mon, I'm going out and I've still got loads to do.'

'Does Sorrel live inside these days?' Hannah asked, intrigued to see Sam carry her across the yard and produce a scoop of grain pellets from a bin inside the barn. He tipped the food into a metal dish, then placed both rabbit and dish inside a roomy hutch. The wooden cage was on a wide shelf about a metre and a half from the floor.

The dwarf Dutch rabbit tucked in greedily, occasionally stopping to take a drink from the water bottle attached to the front netting of the hutch.

'I just said she did, didn't I?' Sam folded his arms and tossed the question back at Hannah.

'Yeah, but why?' She reacted slowly to give Helen chance to smarten Titch up.

'Because of the fox, of course!'

'A fox? Here at Crackpot Farm?'

'Didn't you know that?' Sam asked scornfully. 'Everyone else on Doveton Fell has heard about the fox that's raiding all the farms.'

'They have?' How come she hadn't, she wondered. But then she realised that the news had given her another new opening. 'What you need is a good, well-trained dog to keep the fox away!'

'Hah!' Sam looked at her out of the corner of his eye. 'You're looking for a home for that dumb pup, aren't you?'

'No – that is – er – I mean, yes, now you come to mention it!' Hannah felt herself blush to the roots of her dark-brown hair.

'Hah!' he said again, as if he wasn't the type who could be easily fooled.

'How did you guess?' Hannah wanted to know. The little bubble of hope that had been rising inside her suddenly popped. Instead of gradually leading up to the idea by singing Titch's praises, Sam had rushed her to the vital question.

'I just did. And you're gonna tell me that the puppy is house-trained, mega-clever and all that.'

'Titch does tricks,' she assured him.

'Ah, but does he catch foxes?' Sam stuck to the point.

'He will do when he's grown a bit,' she promised, noting that Helen and Titch had appeared at the door. The puppy looked perky, and was carrying the stick which Hannah and then Sam had thrown for him. 'Do you want to see him do a trick?'

'Go on then,' Sam tutted. 'Like, impress me – NOT!'

Helen took this as her cue to come forward and throw herself into one of her favourite roles. 'Lay-dee and gen'leman!' she announced in her loud circus voice. 'I proudly present to you Mister Titch, the Amazing Performing Puppy!'

'Just make him do the trick,' Sam grunted sourly.

Helen tutted and tossed her head. 'Here, Titch!' she called.

The puppy ran acros the open barn, loudly clattering the stick against solid objects in his way.

From inside her hutch, a startled Sorrel thumped on the floor with her big back feet.

'Ouch! Sam yelled as Titch whacked the stick against his leg.

'Drop it!' Helen ordered.

Titch whirled round and whacked Sam's other leg.

'Ouch!' He hopped from one foot to the other. 'Watch it. I'm supposed to be playing cricket this afternoon!'

Thinking that Sam wanted to join in some fun and games, Titch dropped the stick at his feet. Then he jumped up at the boy, caught him off balance and made him stagger back towards Sorrel's hutch.

Thump-thump-thump! The rabbit panicked. The hutch rocked.

'Whoa!' Hannah and Helen cried, darting forward to steady the hutch. Titch and his stick got tangled up between their legs and they landed in a heap on top of Sam.

'Ouch!'

'Ouch!'

'Ouch!'

And that was it as far as Sam was concerned. It was 'no thanks' to the puppy at Crackpot Farm – fox or no fox.

'Maybe we should've tried harder to persuade the Lawsons to take Titch,' Hannah mused. She sat on the grass at the edge of Doveton village cricket pitch, thoughtfully making a long daisy chain.

Their dad was playing for the local team, along with Luke Martin, Dan Stott and, of course, Sam Lawson.

'No chance,' Helen said glumly. She remembered how Sam's mum had rushed out of the house at the sound of the yells from the barn. There'd been a tangle of arms, legs, sticks and one squashed brown-and-black pup underneath the mass of bodies. Carrie Lawson had pulled poor Titch out and made sure he was all in one piece.

'We'd quite like to adopt him, all things being equal,' she'd told Helen and Hannah when she'd finally managed to make sense of their garbled tale about Fred and Hilda Hunt, Dorothy and Olive White and all the rest. 'It's true that a dog would be useful around here,' she'd agreed.

Titch had wriggled in her arms and licked her hands.

'He likes you!' Hannah had pointed out shyly.

'He likes the sugar on my hands from the biscuits I've been baking!' Carrie had laughed. 'But listen, girls, I'm sorry we can't give Titch a home, much as I might like to.'

Sam had stood smugly shrugging his shoulders.

Hannah and Helen had looked from one to the other.

'Sam and I are going to be away for five weeks this summer,' Carrie had explained. 'We plan to stay with my sister in Florida. So it wouldn't be fair to take on a puppy and then almost straight away have to put him in kennels all the time we're on holiday.'

It had been a good reason, the twins had had to admit. They'd come away from Crackpot Farm feeling dreadfully downhearted, not even bothering to find an answer to Sam's parting shot.

'Five weeks at Disneyland!' he'd crowed after them. 'Oh, and by the way, I've been meaning to ask – can you two look after Sorrel while I'm away?'

'No. I'd rather – I'd rather . . . eat cabbage than ask Sam Lawson to do us a favour ever again!' Now Helen concentrated hard to think of something she hated doing the most. Then she picked a single blade of grass, put it between her thumbs and blew through the gap to make a shrill squawk. Titch pricked up his floppy ear and yelped in surprise.

'Quiet down there!' Mr Winter called from his seat in the official scorer's hut. His grey moustache bristled and the brass buttons on his navy blue blazer gleamed. 'Don't you know there's a serious cricket match going on here?'

Always the head teacher, always barking the orders, always handing out the score. Even Titch fell silent and Helen chucked away her blade of grass.

'Fifty-seven for four,' Cecil Winter noted on his sheet. He passed Hannah a large black card through the hatch in his hut. It had a white '7' printed on it. 'Hang that on the scoreboard,' he ordered. 'Since you girls are sitting there idle, you might as well make yourselves useful!'

Five

'That's sixty-eight for five!' Mr Winter noted the Doveton team score and handed Hannah another card.

On the pitch, Sam Lawson swung his bat. The ball shot between the fielder's legs and reached the boundary close to where Helen sat with Titch.

'Four runs!' the umpire signalled.

'Seventy-two for five,' the ex-head-teacher noted.

'Nice one, Sam. Keep it up!' People in the small crowd clapped and cheered their team on.

'*Yip! Yip!*' Titch made as if to chase the hard red leather ball, until Helen grabbed his collar and held him back.

'If you can't control that dog you'd better take it home!' Mr Winter growled his boring complaint from inside his hut.

Helen huffed. 'We're off to the pavilion,' she told Hannah. 'Sam's mum made those biscuits for team refreshments. I'm gonna see if there are any spares.'

Hannah watched her pick Titch up and wander round the edge of the field towards the big green-and-white pavilion. 'Thanks very much for landing me with Mr Winter!' she muttered.

'Seventy-four for five!' the scorer announced. 'Come along, Helen, here's a nice number four for you to display!'

Hannah weighed up whether or not to tell the old man that he'd got the wrong twin. She decided not to bother.

'Eighty-one for six! . . . ninety-three for seven . . . owzat! . . . No ball! . . . LBW! . . . Leg slip and silly mid-off . . .' All through the long afternoon, Hannah had to put up with the mysterious cricketing terms while Helen and Titch played happily behind the pavilion.

'Thank you, Helen, you did very well!' Mr Winter told Hannah when he emerged from his tiny hut. The Doveton team was all out at last for 177, and Sam Lawson, the only batsman left in, was striding awkwardly towards the pavilion, his legs encased in thick padding.

'Is it time for refreshments?' Hannah asked hopefully.

'Yes, of course, I forgot!' Realising that she must be thirsty, Mr Winter led the way, marching army style across the middle of the pitch.

'Could Helen – er, Hann – erm, I mean my sister, have a drink too?' Hannah asked.

The old man said yes, provided they kept the puppy outside the pavilion. 'Hygiene rules and regulations,' he pointed out. 'Never allow animals where there are foodstuffs. Remember that, Helen!'

He left her waiting on the veranda, where the twins' dad was sitting back in his chair with his feet resting on the rail, deep in conversation with Jack Steele. Both men were dressed in white, taking a rest from the heavy responsibility of playing for Doveton.

'Manchester, you say?' The young farmer was considering David's news about the White sisters.

Helen sat down with Hannah on the wide wooden steps and listened in.

'Manchester's not exactly what Mandy and I had in mind for Titch,' Jack said slowly.

The girls nodded their heads vigorously but didn't dare to interrupt.

'On the other hand, I suppose that if these ladies are offering him a good home, there's no real reason why he shouldn't go and live there.'

Hannah and Helen shook their heads and frowned. *No!* they insisted silently.

Titch lay on the step between them, snatching a quick half-time snooze.

'Mary's not certain that Dorothy White will come back with a definite yes,' David warned. 'But so far, it's the only interest we've had from the advert, and we should know for sure by Thursday of this week.'

'Orange juice!' Mr Winter announced from the doorway, holding a glass in each hand. 'Hannah, dear,' he said to Helen. 'Just pop inside and fetch the bowl of water for the puppy. I left it on the draining-board by the sink.'

Surprised by the kind gesture, Helen ran inside

to fetch Titch's drink. She'd slopped and spilled half of it by the time she'd got back outside but luckily there was still enough left.

'Never let a puppy go without water,' the ex-head-teacher instructed as she set down the bowl on the step. 'And never ever leave them inside a car in hot weather.'

'He must think we're stupid!' Helen hissed as the old man disappeared back inside the pavilion.

Hannah shrugged. She watched Titch wake up, then immediately lap the water. 'I reckon he means well.'

There was a silence, except for the puppy's eager lapping from the bowl.

'Mr Winter does know a lot about dogs,' Hannah said after a while.

'He knows everything about everything,' Helen pointed out, slow to pick up Hannah's drift. She leaned back on the step and tilted her face towards the spring sunshine. 'Like Sam!'

'He must be really lonely without Puppy,' Hannah went on. 'Think how quiet his house must be. And he has no one to take for walks.'

By this time, David and Jack had tuned into the

girls' conversation. They saw the light go on inside Helen's head.

'You mean, Mr Winter and Titch? – Oh no! – No way!' Helen cried, sitting bolt upright.

'Why not?' Hannah frowned. 'He could be the very person we've been looking for. Think about it. He did own a dog until recently.'

'Not a proper dog!' Helen objected. Puppy had been a snappy, yappy little cairn terrier with a hairy face, rather like his owner's, and the same bossy bad temper.

'No, think!' Hannah leaned forward. 'Mr Winter lives right here in Doveton. If he had Titch, we could visit every day on our way to school. We could even take him walks and stuff!'

'Yeah, but Mr Winter – Cecil!' Helen couldn't get used to the idea of the strict old man looking after the funny, tumbling, clumsy little dog. 'Before we knew it, he'd be teaching Titch to count to ten and say his ABC!'

David and Jack laughed.

'Well, anyway, I imagine you would have your work cut out trying to persuade "sir" to give a little rascal like Titch a permanent home,' Jack said. 'So I wouldn't bank on it if I were you.'

But the twins' dad begged to differ. 'Oh, I don't know,' he argued, studying the determined light in Hannah's eyes. 'When my daughters make up their minds to help an animal in distress, there's nothing smaller than a jumbo jet that can stand in their way!'

'Are you sure you don't want anything from the shop?' Hannah asked sweetly.

It was first thing Monday morning and Mr Winter had answered her knock on his door with a suspicious frown.

'No, thank you!' The old man kept his security chain firmly fastened and peered through the narrow gap at the twins. 'I shall be going there myself later this morning.'

'But we could save you the trouble!' Helen said cheesily, her mouth stretched in a wide, false smile. *Cheese-cheese-cheese*. This was another of Hannah's brilliant ideas rapidly coming to nothing.

'Let's be really helpful to Mr Winter!' she'd suggested after the cricket match had ended in a narrow victory for the home side. She'd spent the entire evening working out how they could worm their way into the pensioner's good books.

'Number one – we take Titch with us everywhere we go from now on,' she'd suggested.

'How come?' Helen had asked.

'So Mr Winter gets used to seeing him around. Once he gets to know Titch, he won't be able to resist.'

'You mean, when we eventually ask him to adopt our puppy?' Helen had slowly warmed to the idea.

'Number two – we make ourselves mega-useful to Mr Winter.'

'Watch out. Hannah's on her charm offensive!' their dad had warned, pretending to duck for cover. 'The poor old guy doesn't stand a chance!'

Hannah had tossed her head. 'Don't listen to Dad!' she'd advised Titch, who had yelped and leaped into her lap. 'Number three – we suck up to Cecil like crazy!'

'Yuck!' Helen had grimaced. She knew that this was going to be a difficult act for her to pull off.

And now that they were actually standing on his doorstep, with Hannah being sickly sweet. Helen felt her stomach churn.

'Are you sure there's nothing we could do?' Hannah cooed. 'Like hoovering your carpets or washing your windows?'

'What's wrong with my windows?' the old man growled, his eyebrows joining in the middle. He was obviously proud of his sparkling clean, tidy, terraced cottage.

'Nothing!' Hannah quickly backed down. 'Maybe we could post some letters for you instead?'

'Ah, now you're talking!' came the brisk response. Mr Winter loosened the chain and opened the door wide. 'As a matter of fact, I have a batch of newsletters to send off to my *Hamster World* readers.'

'Great!' Hannah was in through the door, pulling Helen and Titch behind her. She knew that Mr Winter didn't own a hamster himself but that he loved being on the *Hamster World* committee and organising everyone.

'Don't let that puppy tread on my carpet with his muddy paws!' the old man snapped.

Helen sighed and picked Titch up. *No chance!* Silently she rated their prospects of success with the grumpy old fogey.

'The readers of *Hamster World* set a lot of store by my newsletters!' Mr Winter instructed Hannah as he handed her a pile of sealed envelopes. 'You must make sure to put the correct stamp on each one and put it carefully into the postbox.'

Hannah promised that not a single newsletter would go astray.

Hamster-geeks! Helen thought. *What next?*

'After we've posted the letters, is there anything else you'd like us to do?' Hannah asked. She'd stood in front of the mirror in her pyjamas the night before and practised fluttering her eyelashes so that she could do it now.

Yuck! Helen's stomach practically tied itself in knots.

('I don't care what it takes!' Hannah had insisted between flutters. 'The important thing is to get Mr Winter to adopt Titch!')

'Hmm . . .' The ex-head-teacher seemed to run through a list of chores in his head. 'How are you with a paintbrush?' he inquired.

'Good!' Hannah assured him. 'We just painted red and white stripes on a pole for a jump for Titch. He does tricks like jumping, begging and fetching. Titch is a Border collie cross,' she told him brightly. 'Border collies are very clever dogs!'

Mr Winter nodded and glanced at Titch, who was snuggled cosily in Helen's arms, looking fluffy and cute. 'The breed has the intelligence of an average three-year-old child,' he confirmed. 'That's why they make such excellent sheepdogs.'

Hannah smiled. This was going better than she'd expected. 'What would you like us to paint?' she asked sweetly.

'The scorer's hut!' Helen groaned. 'Nice one, Hann. This is gonna take us all day!'

'So?' Armed with paintbrushes and green woodstain, Hannah led the way to the cricket pitch on the outskirts of Doveton. 'Mr Winter did promise to keep an eye on Titch for us while we do the job, didn't he?'

'I s'pose so.' Helen knew it could be bonding time for pooch and Cecil. On the other hand, if Titch misbehaved inside Mr Winter's squeaky-clean house . . .

'And he said he'd be along later to see how we were getting on.' Hannah swung through the gate and strode across the pitch towards the hut. Soon she and Helen would be sloshing woodstain on to the shabby exterior, making it look as good as new.

Shake-stir-dip and slap! Helen swiftly got into the swing and forgot her doubts. Painting was good fun. She painted squiggles and daubs on the old wooden walls, then drew a face, while Hannah worked neatly on the door and window frame.

'Look at this, Hann!' Helen stood back to admire her works of art. There was a clown's face and a stick-man, plus a crooked star shape.

Hannah glanced round the corner. 'Hey, quick!' she gasped as she saw a figure approaching in the distance. 'Mr Winter's coming!'

Slosh-slosh! They covered the daubs before he arrived with Titch on a lead which they'd never seen before.

'This belonged to Puppy,' he explained. 'Waste not, want not, eh? I knew it was bound to come in useful.'

Hannah raised her eyebrows and looked gleefully at Helen. *Is this plan working well, or what?*

'Has Titch been good while you've been looking after him?' Helen asked innocently. She did a pretty mean eyelash flutter all of her own.

'Naturally he's been good,' the old man said in a smug voice. 'There aren't many dogs who dare to misbehave when I'm around!'

Hannah's grin turned to a worried frown. What did this mean? Had Mr Winter been too strict with the playful pup?

But Titch didn't seem upset or sorry for himself. Rather, he waited calmly to be let off the lead then went rooting nosily in the nearby hedge bottom.

For a while Helen and Hannah painted busily, until a sharp bark from Titch attracted their attention.

'What is it?' Helen put down her brush and went to investigate. She found the puppy tugging at an upright piece of wood that had been pushed firmly into the ground. A second, shorter length of wood was nailed to the first in the shape of a cross.

'Oh my!' Mr Winter panicked when he saw what Titch was doing. 'Stop him!'

So Helen made him let go while Hannah ran to help. Together, they straightened the cross then read the letters carefully carved into the surface. The name made them step back quickly. 'We're so sorry!' Hannah exclaimed, her face red with

embarrassmrent. 'Titch didn't realise . . .'

Mr Winter sighed then nodded. 'No, of course not. He wouldn't understand that I buried Puppy here. How could he?'

'It's OK, Titch didn't damage it!' Helen reassured him. The little grave by the hedge was planted with primroses which blossomed pale yellow in the shadow.

'I know people call me an old softie,' Mr Winter confessed, his voice low and softer than usual. 'But over the years this became Puppy's favourite spot. He would lie here watching the cricket while I kept the score. Those are some of my happiest memories . . .'

As he faltered, Hannah and Helen felt their eyes mist up. Even Titch lay on the grass and looked subdued.

Then the ex-head-teacher in Cecil Winter reasserted itself. 'No good wallowing in sadness!' he said briskly. 'We have to get on with life. So let's see what kind of a job you two have been making of my scorer's box!'

Six

'Say that again!' Hannah and Helen's mum demanded as she bundled them into the back of the car.

Titch already sat on the seat, coat brushed and silky, looking all innocent with his smiley face and lopsided ears.

'I said, Mr Winter is really sweet!' Hannah repeated stoutly.

'Ha-ha!' Helen pretended to fall about laughing as she climbed into the car.

'*Sweet?*' Mary echoed, casting a doubtful glance at the twins' dad.

David stood in the doorway with Speckle, ready to wave everyone off for the day. 'Is she talking about

69

the same grumpy, harrumphy old Cecil that we know and love?' he inquired with a choking cough and a grin.

'It's because he made a grave for Puppy and carved his name on a little wooden cross,' Helen told them. 'We saw it in the cricket field yesterday.'

'Aah!' Her mum gave a wistful sigh. 'I agree with Hannah – that's really sweet.'

'Touching,' David admitted. 'And quite sad.'

'But Cecil won't be sad for long,' Helen insisted, hauling Hannah into the car, slamming the door and talking through the open window. 'Not if Hannah has anything to do with it.'

'Ah yes, the charm offensive to make him adopt Titch. How's it going?' David asked.

Helen glanced at Hannah. 'Shall we give him the bad news or the good news?'

'Bad news first.' Hannah remembered the old man's reaction as he'd checked their slapdash work on his precious scorer's hut. His face had turned bright red, then paled and changed to a shade of sickly yellow. 'Let's just say we won't win any prizes for painting huts,' she said quietly. 'Mr Winter told us that a monkey with a brush could have done better. He took over from us and finished it himself.'

Their mum started the engine, in a rush to drop the twins off in the village then drive over to Nesfield to open the café. 'Whoops, write fifty lines and stay in after school!' she said. 'So what's the good news?'

'Mr Winter gave Titch Puppy's old lead,' Helen explained, pulling it out of her pocket to show them. We reckon it's a hopeful sign. What d'you think?'

Mary blew a goodbye kiss to David, then drove slowly into the lane. 'Difficult to judge,' she answered. 'I think it could still go either way with Cecil.'

'He'll say yes!' Hannah insisted. The more she said it, both to herself and out loud, the more likely it was to come true.

'Meanwhile, Dorothy White has been on the phone again.' Their mum quietly sprang the news on them as they coasted downhill. 'She tells me she's almost sure that her sister will come round to the idea of having a puppy, and she wanted to check that Titch was still without a home.'

'Oh no!' Helen cried. Suddenly it seemed urgent to get Mr Winter to say yes. Today was Tuesday. Their deadline was Thursday. That left forty-eight hours to persuade 'sweet' old Mr Winter to offer Titch a home.

Beside her on the back seat, Hannah stared grimly out of the window at the sheep grazing in the fields of Lakeside Farm. She was thinking her own anxious thoughts.

'Here we are, girls!' Mary told them as she pulled up at the kerb outside Mr Winter's house. 'Day two of the charm offensive, as your dad calls it. What's the plan for today?'

Helen lifted Titch out of the car and set him down on the pavement. 'Gardening,' she said, squaring her shoulders and preparing for a morning of digging, clipping, raking and pruning. Charlie Dimmock, eat your heart out!

'Now, this is a flower and this is a weed!' Mr Winter gave Helen and Hannah a first lesson in botany. 'We call this an iris and this nasty purple stuff is rosebay willow-herb. It spreads its seeds everywhere. A gardener's life is a constant battle against it!'

'You want us to dig up the herby stuff?' Helen double-checked. She didn't want any more disasters

72

like yesterday. Today they had to get everything exactly right.

The old man was dressed for work in shirtsleeves, baggy cord trousers and green wellies. He wore a squashed, crumpled fisherman's hat to protect his head from the bright sun. 'That's correct,' he said. 'Dig it out by the roots, put it into the wheelbarrow, then take it round the side of the house and tip it on to the compost heap.'

No more nasty rosebay-blah-blah! Thinking that it might be worthwhile to invent a ray gun that zapped weeds instead of having to go to the trouble of digging them up, Helen daydreamed while Mr Winter droned on.

Moving down the side of the house to show them the compost heap, he pointed out tulips, primroses and bluebells which grew under the two apple-trees on his back lawn.

'Is a bluebell a weed or a flower?' Hannah did her best to show polite interest. Secretly, she wondered how they would manage to make Titch understand the difference once they started work. The puppy was bound to want to dig alongside them. For the moment, however, he was happy rooting around under the nearest tree.

'We would class a bluebell as a wild flower,' the old man explained. He came out with a weird Latin name. 'I do like to see natural areas in gardens. Did you know that the countryside is in grave danger of losing many of its most common species of wild flowers, such as cowslips, due to modern farming methods?'

Helen and Hannah managed to look suitably serious.

Let's dig! Helen thought. *At this rate, we'll know loads about wild flowers, but we'll never get any work done.*

Mr Winter unlocked the door of his garden shed and produced two small trowels for the girls to use. 'If in doubt, come and ask before you dig,' he suggested. 'I'll take the puppy into the house with me, so he can't get up to mischief.'

Hannah gave Helen a small secret grin. 'His name's Titch,' she reminded the starchy ex-schoolteacher.

Titch heard, pricked his ears and trotted towards them, sitting quietly between the twins and looking up with interest at Mr Winter's twitching moustache.

'Hm, Titch, eh?' The old man considered the cute little dog.

'He does tricks,' Helen said proudly. 'Watch him sit up and beg. Come on, Titch, beg!'

On cue, Titch raised his front paws.

'Very good!' Mr Winter was impressed. His voice softened as he leaned over and patted the puppy's head. 'Who deserves a treat for being such a good boy?'

Titch dropped down on to all fours and wagged his tail.

'Come along then.' Turning for the house, Mr Winter led the way with Titch trotting along obediently behind.

'Yes!' Helen gloated. 'Major bonding time, or what!'

Hannah nodded then set to with her trowel. 'Didn't I tell you he was a sweet old man behind all that gruff stuff?'

For a while they weeded and carted the rubbish to the compost heap, growing warm enough to take off their sweatshirts and work in T-shirts. They felt the hot sun on their backs as they dug up worms and unearthed straggly roots of the unwanted weed.

'What about dandelions?' Hannah asked, pausing at a bright yellow, pom-pommy flower head. 'Weeds or flowers?'

'Weeds,' Helen decided, digging at one, pulling and snapping the root in two. 'Oops!'

'Dig deeper,' Hannah suggested, straightening up to ease her back. She glanced at the house and through the open french window saw Mr Winter giving Titch lessons in sit-up-and-beg. The method included the use of a tasty, bone-shaped dog biscuit held between the fingers just out of the puppy's reach.

'This root goes down for ever!' Hannah complained. She was on her hands and knees, turfing earth out of the deepening hole when she hit a rock with the trowel and bent the metal tip. 'Oops!' she said again, this time with an embarrassed giggle.

As she struggled to bend the tip back into shape, she sensed a shadowy figure slink through the hedge and make silently for the patch of bluebells growing under Mr Winter's apple-tree. A first she didn't register anything except a slim creamy body and long black tail but a second glimpse of staring blue eyes and long whiskers told her that it was Luke's cat. Sophie had come to pay them an unexpected visit.

('OK, so I was slow to react!' Hannah admitted later. 'But I wasn't concentrating. I was trying to fix the stupid spade-thing, wasn't I!')

The Siamese cat stared at Helen and Hannah hard at work in Mr Winter's garden. She emerged from the patch of bluebells with her haughty, head-in-the-air walk. Daintily she picked up her black feet and paraded across the lawn in full view.

'*Grrrrr-rrrrrufffffff!*' A whirlwind of black-and-brown fur flew out of the house and launched itself at Sophie.

'*Yeeee-owwwwwl!*' The cat arched her back and stood her ground.

'Come back!' Mr Winter called from his french window. He saw the puppy trample through his tulips and splat his primroses. 'Come here, or else!'

'*Grrrrr!*' Titch eyeballed Sophie. But the moment he came into contact with that violent violet gaze, his nerve went. '*Yip-yip!*' he cried feebly, backing down behind Hannah, then scratching furiously at the soil to hide himself in Helen's freshly dug hole.

'Stop that!' Helen begged, trying in vain to pull the puppy out. He was scrabbling up tulip bulbs and whole primrose plants in his panic.

Sophie saw Titch's front end disappear down the hole. She tossed her elegant head and prowled on, tail flicking, whiskers twitching.

'It's a disgrace!' Mr Winter stormed out of the house and stared at his poor, ruined flowers. Scarlet tulip petals were strewn over his neat lawn, pale yellow primroses were trampled underfoot. 'People who can't train their dogs shouldn't be allowed to keep them. And certainly they shouldn't bring them into other people's garden to wreak havoc!'

'*Yip!*' Poor Titch yelped as Helen at last managed to drag him from the hole. His face was covered in soil, his body trembled. Then he hid himself against Helen's T-shirt and whimpered.

'It wasn't Titch's fault,' Hannah tried to say. She was frantically grabbing uprooted flowers and trying to replant them. The tulips were beyond rescue but the clumps of primroses seemed likely to survive.

The old teacher stood with his hands on his hips, staring at the deep hole and mound of earth. 'No, it's my fault entirely,' he began severely, 'for trusting you two with my lovely garden and expecting you to be able to train some sense into that puppy!'

'But it's not so bad!' Helen argued, quickly filling the hole with one hand while she held a squirming Titch with the other. 'If you take him back into the house, Hannah and me will soon sort this lot!'

'Hannah and *I*!' Mr Winter corrected severely. '*Hannah and I will sort it out!*' He shook his head to show them that standards in schools had dropped dramatically since his days. He glowered at the twins with small, mean eyes that had almost disappeared beneath the bushy grey brows. 'In any case, if you truly believe that I would ever let that muddy little vandal set foot back inside my nice clean house, then let me tell you, Helen and Hannah Moore, you have another thing coming!'

Seven

'OK, so it's a setback,' Hannah admitted later that day. She, Helen and Titch had made a quick exit from Mr Winter's ruined garden and even she had to recognise that their road into the old man's good books was littered with booby-traps. Now she sat on the gate at Home Farm, waiting for their mum to come home from work.

'It's more than a setback!' Helen protested. '*Total disaster*, more like.'

Hannah tutted. 'You always exaggerate.'

'Oh yeah! What does "Never set foot inside my house ever again!" sound like to you, Dad?' Helen appealed for a referee. 'Is that a little or a big problem, coming from the person who we want to adopt Titch?'

'Pretty major, if you ask me. Sorry, Hann.' David had just finished hauling heavy bales of straw down from the top of the stack in the barn. He was dusty and dishevelled, still wearing the jumper that had been stained pink during an earlier 'setback' with playful Titch.

Helen nodded at Hannah. *Told-you-so!* 'D'you still think of him as sweet old Cecil?' she asked.

Hannah kicked her heels stubbornly against the bar of the gate. 'Yeah, he was giving Titch treats, remember. Until Sophie came along and spoiled everything.'

' "Hannah and I!" ' Helen quoted the old man in a pompous voice. ' "Puppy and I!" '

'You sound like the queen,' Hannah snapped.

'Ooh, tetchy!'

'Big-head.'

'Twit.'

'Girls!' their dad warned.

'Well!' they both said. Hannah stared down the lane while Helen went and sat on the swing under the chestnut-tree.

David stooped to pick up Titch who had been chasing blossom petals across the yard. 'So I take it you've given up on finding him a home with Cecil?' he asked them. 'And this little chap will have to go off to Manchester with Olive and Dorothy?'

'Yes!' Helen confirmed, swinging angrily under the new green leaves. 'Hannah and ME tried, but it didn't work out.'

There was silence from Hannah while her thoughts whirled. Sure they'd tried – Mr Winter, Sam Lawson, Luke, Fred and Hilda, the Stotts – she practically ran through the whole of Doveton village, remembering how hard they'd worked to find a home for Titch. But maybe not hard enough . . .

'So we'd better make the most of you for the next day or so,' their dad murmured to Titch.' Because after that you're likely to be a long way away, getting used to a whole new world!'

Ouch! Hannah felt the comment drive into her like a knife.

'Here comes Mum!' Helen shouted from her high vantage point. The swing plummeted and she jumped off at precisely the right moment.

Soon the car came trundling up to the gate, its

old engine coughing and spluttering after the hilly drive from Nesfield.

'Why the gloom and doom?' Mary asked immediately as she stepped out of the car. One quick glance at Helen and Hannah had told her that the girls weren't happy.

' 'S not fair!' Hannah wailed. 'Mr Winter blamed Titch for ruining his garden . . . !'

'. . . And it was Sophie's fault!' Helen added. This was when she admitted to herself that, OK, she'd been slow to act. Yes, she'd seen the darned cat slinking through the shadows and she'd done nothing to chase Sophie away. So she didn't say this out loud – so what?

'Helen, Hannah!' Their dad stepped in to hand Titch to their mum, then unload her bag from the car. 'Let your poor mum get in through the door and put her feet up with a cup of tea before you bombard her with the day's disasters!'

'Setbacks!' Hannah contradicted stubbornly, and this time Helen didn't argue.

They trailed into the house together, brightening for a few seconds when their mum stopped to put Titch down in the hallway and turned to them. 'Don't worry, all is not lost,' she told them with a tired smile. 'I know you don't want Titch to go to Manchester, and as luck would have it, I've had a couple more inquiries today about our advert.'

Hannah gasped and Helen asked, 'Who?'

'Wait, wait, wait! Let me call Mandy and Jack with the latest developments,' Mary protested. 'If you listen, you'll find out everything you want to know.'

The girls stood impatiently while their mum punched in the Keld House numbers.

'Oh, Jack – hello. Yes, it's Mary. Good news on the puppy front. You'll be pleased to hear that two more families have expressed interest in giving Titch a home.'

Helen held her breath. *Doveton!* she prayed. *Let it be someone living close by. And if not Doveton, then Nesfield at the very furthest!*

'One inquiry came from a young Scottish couple. They live way up in the Highlands . . . yes, just visiting the Lakes . . . that's right.'

Scotland! Helen's heart sank. Her mum might as well have said the moon.

Hannah hung her head and listened on.

'The second people were in The Curlew this

afternoon and they sounded very very keen. They're from Yorkshire – a little ex-mining town in the south. I must say, they seemed nice.'

Yorkshire! Hannah sighed. A mining town. Nice people or not, she definitely didn't like the sound of that.

Sadly she and Helen retreated from the hallway, leaving their mum to arrange for Jack to come and meet all three groups of prospective owners during Thursday lunch-time.

'Manchester!' Helen began as they trudged outside and wandered towards the field, where Solo and Stevie stood with their heads over the wall. She climbed up and absent-mindedly stroked the pony.

'The Highlands of Scotland!' Hannah muttered gloomily. Stevie the donkey head-butted her, demanding attention. 'Or Yorkshire!' Stevie's greeting had pushed her backwards and landed her in the ditch. Still she climbed the wall again and stroked his knobbly, hairy head.

Manchester, Scotland, Yorkshire – in less than two days time, Titch would end up in one of these three distant places.

'Unless we try one more time with Cecil,' Helen

muttered as she and Hannah finally finished their chores and dragged themselves to bed after what was turning out to be a really bad day.

'What did you say?' Hannah asked. She was brushing her teeth in the bathroom and the sound of the running tap had partly drowned out Helen's voice.

Helen wandered in, already dressed in her pyjamas with her feet snuggled into her favourite rabbit slippers. 'I said: we-could-try-one-more-time-with-Mr-Winter,' she repeated rapidly. This was backing down big-time, but what else could she do?

Hannah almost bit off the head of her toothbrush in surprise. 'Try again?' True, they had one more day, but when it came to it, did they have enough grit and determination?

Just then Titch charged into the crowded bathroom and launched an attack on Helen's slippers. He grabbed a furry ear and twisted it, then grappled the whole head, including Helen's toes snuggled inside.

Helen struggled free and Hannah picked the puppy up to scold him. She held him up in the air and shook him gently. 'No!' she chided. 'We don't

pounce on small furry things – that includes rabbit slippers and Siamese cats!'

Titch's wide mouth smiled down at them. His brown eyes sparkled.

It was the look that melted both their hearts.

Hannah took a deep breath. 'Right!' she said. 'Tomorrow we try again!'

'Half a league, half a league,
  Half a league onward . . .
  Into the valley of Death
  Rode the six hundred!'

The twins' dad quoted an ancient poem as he dropped the twins and Titch outside the village shop early next morning.

'You what?' Helen quizzed.

'Into the valley of Death!' he insisted. 'It's famous – "The Charge of the Light Brigade". Ask Mr Winter when you see him! Oh and by the way, it's "pardon", not "You what"!'

'Huh,' Helen grunted. 'Bye, Mister Schoolteacher Dad!'

'Yeah, bye!' Hannah waved him off, eager to follow her new brilliant idea from the night before.

'I wonder if Sophie often goes into Mr Winter's garden?' she'd mused in the darkness of the bedroom.

'Spect so,' Helen had mumbled, already half asleep.

'Yeah, his house is just down the road from Luke's shop.' Hannah had pictured the bold cat strolling through the row of back gardens towards the cricket field where he was often to be found sunning himself on the steps of the pavilion. 'Hmmm . . .' she'd murmured.

But Helen hadn't stayed awake to hear more.

Now, though, she agreed with Hannah that this was a good place to begin the third day of their Keep-Titch-in-Doveton campaign. 'I'll stay outside with Titch. You go and check things out with Luke.'

The *ting-a-ling* of the doorbell took Hannah into the small shop where Luke was already busy. 'Aha!' he said when he spotted Hannah. 'I see you're on a mission.'

She gave a puzzled frown.

'This isn't just a social call,' he explained. 'I can tell by the look on your face.'

'In that case, yes, you're right. I need to ask you something about Sophie.'

'Fire away!' Luke invited, pretending to be nervous. 'What's she been up to now?'

'She's not exactly been up to anything,' Hannah hedged, knowing how fond Luke was of his elegant cat.

'Has she been showing off again?'

'No, honest. But what I want to know is – er – does she often go walkabout?'

'Ah, you've been talking to dear old Cecil!' Luke surmised. 'Has he been complaining about my lovely pride and joy again?'

'Not exactly.' Hannah stammered in surprise at the automatic connection that Luke had made. 'Why should Mr Winter complain about Sophie?'

'Simple – because she regularly goes and digs holes in his garden,' Luke explained. 'You know cats – they're clean creatures when it comes to – er – hygiene matters.'

Hannah nodded hastily.

'Well, since Puppy passed away, Sophie seems to have taken to choosing Cecil's flower-beds to do her – er – business in. Maybe it's because the soil is so soft and crumbly . . .'

Another nod from Hannah came before her lightning exit. 'Thanks, Luke!' she gasped, leaving him standing.

'What did I say?' he wondered as the bell tinkled and the door crashed shut.

'Hi, Mr Winter. We came to ask you about a famous poem,' Helen practised in a polite voice as she held Titch on a lead down Main Street. She and Hannah had agreed that it would be best not to jump straight into the topic of puppies, cats and holes in the garden. They'd guessed that the old teacher would be pleased to be asked a question about poetry. 'It's about the valley of Death and the six hundred.'

Meanwhile, Hannah rehearsed her own part, once Helen had softened the old man up. 'Mr Winter, just think how useful it would be to have a dog in the house again. I mean, as soon as Sophie realises that Titch lives here, she and all the cats in the neighbourhood would stay away from your garden!'

She would look winningly at Mr Winter and this would be Helen's cue to come in again.

'And Titch really likes you!' she would insist. She would hold the puppy up with his bright eyes and smiling mouth. 'Look how pleased he is to see you!'

This was the exact plan, carefully laid out while they sat on the bench outside Luke's shop.

'Right!' Hannah had said at last. She'd taken a deep breath, stood up and set off down the street.

'Right!' Helen had echoed. *Now or never*.

They reached the ex-head-teacher's house at the end of the terrace. The gate clicked open as Hannah pressed the catch. Then they walked up the narrow path to the front door . . .

Eight

Helen's mouth felt dry. Mr Cecil's angry voice rang in her ears. He'd called Titch a "muddy little vandal" and sworn never to let him set foot inside his nice clean house ever again.

Yet here they were – Titch, Hannah and herself – marching up his garden path as bold as you like. *Wow, we've got a nerve!* she thought. She swallowed hard and waited for Hannah to knock on the old man's door.

Will Mr Winter forgive Titch? Hannah wondered. She glanced down at the puppy's smiling face, then seized the polished brass knocker. To her surprise, the door swung open.

'That's weird,' Helen said. Mr Winter was the type of person who would always keep his front door firmly locked.

'Shall I knock?' Hannah wasn't sure what to do next.

Helen nodded. 'He must be in there. He wouldn't have gone out and left his door open.'

So Hannah held the door and rapped the knocker.

Rat-tat-tat! The sound echoed down Mr Winter's narrow hallway. Titch sat on the doorstep, ears pricked as the girls listened for footsteps.

But there was no response to their knock.

'Maybe he's in the back garden,' Helen suggested, scooting down the side of the house. She soon reappeared with a shake of her head. 'Nope.'

'Hmm.' Hannah knocked again. As she rapped the knocker, the door swung further open.

A grandfather clock ticked loudly at the end of the narrow hall. The brass pendulum gleamed in a ray of sunlight. Closer to the door, a wooden umbrella-stand containing a black, rolled-up umbrella had its place under a row of coat-hooks, from which hung Mr Winter's gardening hat and a pale straw panama.

'This isn't like Cecil to leave the safety chain off,' Helen muttered. She peered down the hall and up the stairs. 'Hello . . . Mr Winter?'

Yet again, there was no answer.

'You don't think he's had an accident?' Hannah whispered, turning to Helen with wide, worried eyes.

'You mean, he could be in there, lying on the floor in the kitchen?' Helen felt a small fear dart through her. You heard of old people falling over and not being able to get up again. Sometimes they lay without help for days on end.

Hannah nodded. She called the old man's name again – louder this time.

Sitting patiently on the doorstep, Titch felt the tension rise. He grew super alert, straining to peer round the edge of the door. Then he yelped and made a dart inside the house.

'Here, Titch!' Hannah cried out. This was nightmare stuff – the puppy bounding down Mr Winter's hallway, probably muddying up the swirly patterned carpet and lunging into the kitchen to grab food from the table!

'*Yip-yip!*' Titch galloped past the umbrella-stand,

reached the grandfather clock, turned round and raced back.

'Good boy!' Hannah heaved a sigh of relief.

'Y'know, this is getting serious,' Helen muttered. 'What d'you say we take a proper look?'

Slowly Hannah nodded. She put Titch on the lead, then all three ventured inside the house.

They trod warily down the hallway, politely calling Mr Winter's name.

Apart from the regular tick of the clock, they were met by silence.

'Try that door!' Hannah whispered, pointing to what she thought must be Mr Winter's sitting-room.

Gingerly Helen pushed it open. The small room was crowded with furniture. A flowery sofa took up the whole of the bay window, then there were two matching chairs and a low coffee table set out with magazines on gardening and hamsters. A crammed bookshelf lined the whole of one wall.

'There's no one in here!' Helen reported with a sigh of relief. But she noticed an array of silver photo-frames displayed along the mantelpiece and she crept in for a closer look. 'Aah!' she whispered. 'Look at these, Hann!'

Keeping Titch on a short lead, Hannah studied the photographs. There was Mr Winter sitting in a fireside chair with Puppy on the rug at his feet, Mr Winter and Puppy at the seaside, a close-up of Puppy wearing a natty tartan leather collar, Puppy snoozing in front of Mr Winter's scorer's hut . . .

'Aah!' Hannah echoed Helen. 'Sad, or what?'

Helen nodded. 'It makes you realise how lonely Mr Winter must be without him.'

'Anyway, he's not here at the moment,' Hannah decided.

Helen thought it was worth checking the rest of the house, so she darted into the kitchen and up the stairs to check the bedrooms. Two minutes later she was back and confirming Hannah's conviction that the house was empty.

'How come he went out without closing the door?' Hannah demanded again. 'Anyone could just walk in off the street!'

'Yeah, like us!' Helen pointed out. She lunged forward to stop Titch from dragging Mr Winter's checked slippers out from under the umbrella-stand. 'Listen, maybe he just popped to the shop.'

Hannah stepped out on to the path, turning to

look up at the neat little end-of-terrace house. 'Maybe,' she answered with a doubtful shrug. 'I suppose we could go and check.'

'So do we close the door after us?' Helen wondered. 'I mean, what if Mr Winter doesn't have his key with him?'

In the end, they decided to close the door but leave it off the latch. Then they hurried back down Main Street towards Luke's shop.

'Wouldn't we have seen Mr Winter on the way here as we were coming in the opposite direction?' Hannah pointed out a flaw in Helen's theory that the old man had popped out on an errand to the only shop in the village.

'Well maybe he forgot he'd left his door open and got dragged into somebody's house for a chat.' Helen stuck to her plan to at least ask Luke if he'd seen Mr Winter lately. 'Wait outside with Titch – I won't be a sec,' she told Hannah as she pushed open the door.

Ting-a-ling! The doorbell announced her entrance but the shop was too full for Luke to look up and greet her. Hilda Hunt was there, looking for a birthday card to send to her sister in Wales. There was a man dressed in walker's gear of orange waterproof jacket, heavy socks and boots, carrying a small rucksack, plus two middle-aged women in fawn jackets, tweedy skirts and flat lace-up shoes.

One of the women was buying postcards and stamps, handing over the money, then asking Luke questions about the area.

'How far are we from Nesfield?' she asked in a precise, high-pitched voice.

Squashed in her corner of the shop and forced to wait, Helen made out the side view of a thin woman with sharp features and thick, short, grey hair.

'You're eight miles from town if you go via the top road over Hardstone Pass,' Luke replied. 'Ten miles if you take the easier valley road.'

The woman nodded and briefly spoke to her companion – also thin, with the same bony nose. 'Olive and I have driven over from Manchester,' she explained. 'We especially wanted to come through Doveton and take a look around.'

'Well, it's a very pretty village,' Luke told her, going on to point out places of interest nearby.

But Helen wasn't listening to his tour guide. Had she heard right? Did the postcard woman call her companion Olive? Had she definitely said that they'd come from Manchester? For a few seconds she completely forgot about the missing Mr Winter and the reason why she'd come. Because, unless she was making a big mistake, she had just walked slap bang into the women who wanted to adopt Titch!

Dorothy White was a persistent type. Although the shop was full, she asked Luke further questions. 'I expect you know the Moore family at Home Farm?' she went on.

'I certainly do,' Luke answered chirpily.

Helen shuffled sideways to hide behind the postcard rack. Even though Hilda gave her a funny look, she was determined to listen in without being seen.

'Are they nice people?' Olive spoke up for the first time. She had a quieter voice than the other woman, but was just as dogged.

'The Moores are great,' Luke assured them. 'Ever since they moved into Home Farm, they've made themselves at home in Doveton. Everyone likes them. They have twin girls, y'know – identical – and the kids are bonkers about animals.'

'You see!' The first woman turned to Olive with a satisfied smile. 'I knew we'd hear nice things about

the family. The mother is a lovely type of person – very caring. I was sure they'd have looked after the puppy well.'

'Is this little Titch you're talking about?' Luke began to take more interest in the conversation.

Olive nodded. 'My sister, Dorothy here, wants us to adopt the puppy. We have to make a decision by tomorrow and I said we had to be absolutely sure that Titch came from a good background. After all, we don't want to take on a problem dog who's been neglected or abused. That's why we were asking you about the Moores.'

Luke smiled reassuringly. 'Oh, you've no worries on that score. And you're quite right to check things out thoroughly. I'd do the same if I were you.'

For a few seconds the two ladies spoke quietly together. It gave Helen time to get over her surprise and gather her thoughts. On the one hand, she blushed with pleased embarrassment to hear Luke sing her family's praises. On the other, she wished like mad that he'd given them a bad report: *Oh no, those people are terrible with animals. They don't have a clue about training dogs. If I were you, I wouldn't touch the puppy with a barge-pole!*

'I understand from Mary Moore that we have competition,' Dorothy White went on in her clear, confident voice. 'There are now two other sets of people who are interested in adopting Titch. So we – Olive and I – thought we would like get in there first by visiting Home Farm today rather than waiting to see the puppy in Nesfield tomorrow lunch-time with the others.'

From behind the rack, Helen gasped. She realised that the sisters wouldn't have to go as far as Home Farm – that as soon as they stepped out of the shop, they would come face to face with Titch and Hannah.

I've gotta get out of here! she said to herself.

So she slipped out from behind the postcards and sidled towards the door. Her getaway was quick and silent, except for the *ting-a-ling* of the doorbell as she exited.

'Hann!' she gasped, almost bursting with the urgency of getting Titch out of sight.

As Hannah jerked up from the seat outside the shop, Titch leaped to his feet. 'What is it? Helen, what's wrong?' she demanded, fearing bad news about poor Mr Winter.

'Don't ask! I'll explain later!' Helen hissed back.

She grabbed Titch's lead from Hannah and began to sprint up the street. 'Come on, Hann!' she yelled over her shoulder. 'Hurry up out of here, or we're dead!'

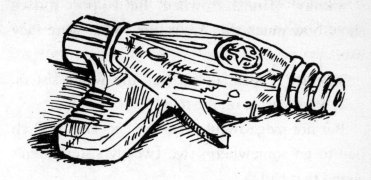

Nine

'If Olive and Dorothy had seen Titch, they'd have fallen in love with him on the spot!' Helen gasped.

Hannah stared at Helen, who had flopped against the garden shed at the back of Mr Winter's house. 'Is that why you just broke the world record for the hundred metres sprint?' Slowly she was piecing together the reason why Helen had made her dash from outside the shop. It had nothing to do with news about the old head teacher after all.

'I'm telling you, it was the sisters from Manchester – here in Doveton – trying to snatch a preview of Titch before the other people have chance to see him!'

'Sneaky!' Hannah frowned. 'But I s'pose it does show how much they want him. What were they like?'

'Tweedy!' Helen summed up the White sisters. 'Like Miss Marple on the telly!'

'But not mega-awful?' Hannah checked. If Titch had to go somewhere, two tweedy sisters didn't sound that bad.

Helen tutted crossly. 'That's not the point. We want Mr Winter to have Titch, not them, remember!'

'Yeah, but . . .' It was Hannah's turn to lose faith in their Keep-Titch-in-Doveton scheme. After all, the Manchester sisters had gone to a lot of trouble to show up early in the village. Meanwhile, Mr Winter was nowhere to be found.

Exasperated, Helen dragged herself to her feet. 'Yeah, but – nothing!' she retorted. 'My guess is that Olive and Dorothy will be heading for Home Farm right this minute. It'll take them maybe half an hour or forty-five minutes to get up there, see Dad, and be told that Titch isn't home and that we have him with us. Then they'll be back down, knocking at Mr Winter's door, looking for him!'

That gave them three-quarters of an hour

maximum to find Cecil and persuade him to adopt Titch. It all had to happen before the sisters had chance to make their offer and whisk the puppy away to the smoky city...

Hannah looked down at Titch, still panting from the race along the street. He looked cute and loveable, lying with his tongue lolling, his head on his paws. She knew right then that it would break her heart never to see him again. 'OK!' she decided, 'let's check along the row of houses to see if Mr Winter is visiting a neighbour. If not, then it's back to Luke's. Come on, Helen, get a move on!'

'No,' they said at number eight. 'No, sorry girls,' at number ten. 'No,' again next door to that. No one had seen Cecil all morning.

'... As a matter of fact, no,' Luke told them, registering mild surprise. 'He hasn't dropped by for his newspaper this morning. That's almost unheard of.'

'He left his front door open, wherever he went,' Hannah told him.

Just then, Titch growled from his spot on the

doorstep as his arch-enemy, Sophie, strolled along the pavement.

The cat flicked the tip of her tail, jumped on to the wall and studied the doves on the roof.

'That reminds me!' Luke said. 'A couple of ladies were in here asking about Titch. Apparently, they've decided to offer him a home and I must say they did seem quite nice . . .'

'Yeah, thanks, Luke. Bye!' Helen gabbled, making her second rapid exit of the day.

Sophie heard the racket made by the jangling doorbell, turned and glared.

'*Yip!*' Titch barked, as fiercely as he could.

Fifteen minutes had gone by, and the twins were no nearer to tracking down Mr Winter, until the neighbour who lived at 12 Main Street beckoned them back. Hannah and Helen knew her as Jill Hartley – a short-sighted, elderly widow with frizzy dyed blonde hair and a liking for bright, flowery blouses.

'I was thinking about what you asked me – y'know, had I seen Cecil?' Mrs Hartley hailed Hannah, who ran along the pavement with Titch in tow. 'I told you no I hadn't, but then seeing Luke's cat pass across my front garden just now reminded me that as a matter of fact I had!'

'You have!' Hannah gasped.

'When? Where?' Helen butted in. This was their first lead and she prayed hard that it would turn out to be a good one.

Jill Hartley was the sort of person who didn't make much sense at the best of times. She muddled things and acted in a dizzy, dithery way – an 'eccentric' type, as the twins' dad would say.

'Hold your horses,' she insisted. 'Sophie – Cecil! Well, that's chalk and cheese. In other words, they don't get on at all well!' She winked at Helen and Hannah as if passing on a well-kept secret.

'We know that but what about it?' Hannah urged.

'Cecil has a water pistol,' Mrs Hartley confided.

A water pistol? Mr Winter? Helen's heart sank. What kind of crazy information was this?

'He keeps it ready on his kitchen windowsill,' Mrs Hartley went on in her rambling way. 'He fills it with soapy water and every time he sees Sophie come into his garden, he grabs the water pistol, dashes out and aims it at the cat!'

Hannah's eyes widened.

'Really and truly! I know you don't believe me, but I've often seen him do it,' the old lady insisted. 'Cats don't like soapy water. I expect the idea is to discourage Sophie from using his garden as a toilet. The only trouble is, Cecil's aim isn't very good!'

Helen got the picture but still didn't see what it had to do with Mr Winter's mysterious disappearance. 'C'mon, Hann!' she urged, tugging at her arm. 'We're running out of time!'

But Hannah resisted. 'Hang on a sec. Mrs Hartley, are you saying that's what Mr Winter was doing when you saw him this morning?'

'Exactly, my dear. Cecil shot out of his front door and fired a jet of water at the poor creature. He missed of course, and the cat fled across the front lawn with Cecil in hot pursuit. I saw the whole thing with my own eyes – Sophie shooting out on to the street, Cecil still running after her with the water pistol in his hand.' Mrs Hartley shook her blonde frizz and scoffed at the memory. 'Last seen heading in a very undignified manner for the cricket field,' she told the twins. 'If I were you, that's the next place I should look.'

* * *

The minutes ticked by.

Hannah, Helen and Titch followed Jill Hartley's advice and headed for the cropped, manicured and rolled pitch at the bottom of the village street.

It was a distance of about a hundred and fifty metres, and they covered it in under thirty seconds. Helen was counting.

'Mr Winter and a water pistol?' Hannah frowned as Helen helped Titch squeeze under the gate into the field. 'That doesn't sound right somehow.'

Helen pictured the crusty old teacher in his navy blue blazer with its brass buttons. He would spy a cat, raise the pistol, aim and fire. *Squirt – plop!* The jet of water would fall short. Mr Winter's moustache and eyebrows would twitch in fury. He would aim again . . . 'I know!' she agreed. 'It sounds more like something Dad would do!'

'Go through, Titch!' Helen shoved the reluctant puppy from behind. Eventually he squeezed under the gate and the twins quickly climbed into the field after him.

The grass spread evenly before them, a white line marking the boundaries, a smooth, almost bald strip in the middle showing where the wicket was. To the right was the big green-and-white pavilion, while across the far side of the field was Mr Winter's newly painted scorer's hut.

'There's no sign of him!' Hannah sighed, scanning the whole ground.

'We might've known Mrs Hartley was talking gobbledegook!' Helen muttered.

'Let's look in the pavilion, just to make sure.'

They ran quickly to the refreshment building, tried the door and found it locked. Titch sniffed at the bottom of the door, followed a scent along the veranda, then hopped down on to the grass. Soon he was scooting off towards the scorer's hut, tail in the air, nose to the ground.

Hannah looked at Helen. 'What d'you think?'

'Might as well follow him,' Helen decided flatly. At this rate, the White sisters would be back in the village before they found any trace of Mr Winter, and it would all be over.

Titch followed a zigzagging course round the edge of the pitch. Once he stopped for a good sniff, turning in small circles, then veering off towards the hut once more.

Following close on the puppy's heels, the

twins inspected the frothy patch of grass that had interested Titch.

'Soap!' Hannah murmured, stooping to pop a shiny, filmy bubble with her fingertip.

Suddenly Jill Hartley's story didn't sound so crazy after all. They hurried to catch up with Titch once more.

The puppy was already sniffing hard round the base of the tiny hut when Hannah and Helen arrived. He put his nose to the bottom of the door, then began to scratch at the new paint.

'D—t —t —t -up scratch -y -ut!' A muffled voice said something unintelligible.

Helen and Hannah whirled round. They looked everywhere without being able to make out where the voice had come from or what it had said.

Excitedly, Titch went on scratching at the door to the hut.

The wooden flap at the front opened fifteen centimetres and two bushy eyebrows and a prickly moustache peered out. 'I said, don't let that puppy scratch my hut!' Mr Winter said in a peeved but embarrassed voice.

* * *

'You must promise not to tell a single soul!' The ex-head-teacher swore Hannah and Helen to secrecy.

The girls had lifted the latch to let him out of the hut and he'd emerged shamefacedly, trying to hide his red plastic water pistol behind his back.

They'd shuffled around and stared at their feet, desperate not to giggle as Mr Winter tried to explain how it had all come about.

'I was creeping up on that darned Siamese cat,' he'd begun. 'I'd been following it all the way down Main Street until it decided to come and scratch at the cricket pitch. Imagine that – a dratted cat digging up the smoothest wicket in Cumbria!'

Hannah had tutted in sympathy. Helen had raised her hand to cover her mouth.

'I decided to employ stealth,' Mr Winter had continued, marching Titch, Hannah and Helen away from the cricket field, back towards his house. All the while, the girls had kept a lookout for the White sisters. So far, it was all clear.

'My plan was to take cover in the hut while the cat scratched,' the old man had told them, slipping the water pistol into the inside pocket of his blazer. 'When she'd finished and was approaching my lookout point, I would be aiming, ready to fire! The only problem was, I didn't securely raise the latch on the door. It clicked down as I entered, and since there's no handle on the inside, unfortunately I was locked in.'

Helen had snuffled to hide a loud guffaw, while Hannah's eyes had grown large and round. Her stomach hurt from trying not to laugh.

'Harrumph!' Mr Winter had glared at them, but had been too ashamed and too grateful to tell them off.

'Titch did really well to find you!' Hannah said, her voice choking.

'Harrumph!' Mr Winter said again.

'Without him, you'd still be locked in the hut!' Helen pointed out.

The old man sniffed grumpily and cast a glance at the puppy, who had roamed up his garden to sniff under the hedge.

'Someone might have come and burgled your house if you'd been locked in any longer,' Hannah added.

'Or you could have stayed in there for ever and starved to death!' Helen's imagination ran riot.

'Nonsense!' Mr Winter mumbled, but he was looking in a soft, misty-eyed way at clever Titch.

Just then, the puppy stood tall and made his hackles rise. He bared his teeth in a sudden snarl.

'What the . . .!' Mr Winter cried, immediately drawing his water pistol and aiming at the hedge bottom.

'*Yeeeowwwwl!*' Sophie's familiar caterwauling cry split the air.

'*Grrrrrr-rrrrgh!*' Titch darted into the hedge, snapped his jaws and closed them on the tip of Sophie's tail.

The cat's cry rose up the scale. '*Yee-owww!*'

Pounce! Titch followed up his guerilla attack on the old enemy. He came down on Sophie's back. The cat struggled free and streaked on to the lawn.

Splurge! – Swoosh! Cecil aimed and fired.

'Good shot!' Hannah cried.

The cat got it on the back of the head.

'*Yeeoww!*' She shot down the side of the house.

Mr Winter beamed. He went right over and picked Titch up. 'Splendid!' he cried as the puppy stretched up and licked his chin. 'This little chap is a real hero! In fact, whenever you and the Steeles are ready to

let him go, he can come and live with me. After I've trained him correctly, Titch and I will be able to maintain this row of gardens as a one hundred per cent cat-free zone!'

'It was your Sophie who clinched it,' Helen admitted to Luke, who had come to visit them at Home Farm that evening. He had joined the Moores and Mandy and Jack Steele over a glass of beer under the blossoming chestnut-tree. 'If Sophie hadn't been a total nuisance at the exact moment when the White sisters arrived back in the village, Cecil would never have changed his mind about Titch in time!'

The grown-ups laughed.

'I'm glad he did!' Hannah sighed, stroking Leila with one hand and Speckle with the other. Both mother and father looked on proudly as Helen prepared Titch to perform his new trick.

This was, in fact, the puppy's last night at Home Farm. First thing tomorrow, they would take his basket and blanket down to Mr Winter's house and sadly but gratefully hand him over to his new owner.

'Well, I'm glad Sophie the show-off comes in useful occasionally!' Luke said cheerfully. 'And you're sure that Dorothy and Olive from Manchester weren't too disappointed?'

'They happened to be peering over the garden wall when Mr Winter splatted Sophie,' Hannah told him. 'They saw how pleased he was that Titch had chased Sophie away, and when he said he wanted to keep Titch, they were pretty good considering they'd come such a long way. Dorothy said they'd soon find another puppy and that they were glad Mr Winter was happy...'

'... Di-dah-di-dah!' Helen sang. 'Actually, I think Olive really fancied Cecil!'

'Helen!' her mum said, pretending to be shocked.

'She invited herself in for tea and cooed over all his old photos of Puppy!' Helen insisted.

'Anyway, everything turned out fine,' David chipped in before Helen stretched her story and had Cecil nicely married off. 'Go on, girls, make Titch show us this new trick before it gets dark!'

So Helen and Hannah led the puppy to the middle of the yard. There was a big audience of the grown-ups, plus Leila and Speckle, plus Solo and Stevie looking over the wall, plus Socks the cat and all the other animals that the twins had given a home to since their move to Home Farm.

'Sit, Titch!' Hannah said, with a nervous catch in her voice. *Don't let us down in front of everyone!*

Titch sat, thank heavens. So Hannah turned to Helen who was to give the next order.

'Spin!' Helen told the obedient puppy.

Titch turned on the spot, chasing his own wagging tail. Once, twice, three, four times he spun round like an aerial acrobat in the spotlight.

'Jump!' Hannah and Helen cried, linking hands to form a cradle.

With a delighted yelp he sprang into their arms. He landed neatly and sat waiting for the applause.

'Magnificent! Bravo! More!' The audience clapped and cheered.

Helen grinned at Hannah as they lowered the puppy to the ground.

'Good boy!' Hannah whispered in his ear.

Titch cocked an ear and gave her his lopsided grin.

Helen stood up and stepped proudly back. 'Lay-dees an' gen'lemen!' she announced in a sing-song voice. What better way to say goodbye to the adorable little clown? 'Here he is, the one and only, the totally a-may-zing Trrricky Titch!'

Another Hodder Children's book

SMARTY THE OUTCAST
Home Farm Twins Christmas Special

Jenny Oldfield

Loyal old Smarty, the pony, has retired from
Manor Farm Riding School and moved to a
new home with the Rooneys. But Helen and
Hannah are worried he is being neglected.
They spot him in a windswept shelter with
no rug and inadequate protection from the
cold winter weather. Should the twins offer
to lend a hand or call in the RSPCA?

**HOME FARM FRIENDS:
A Short Story Collection**

Jenny Oldfield

Old friends – new adventures! Speckle the sheepdog in a watery challenge; Scott the Shetland pony in a hospital drama; Stanley the hamster in another daring episode and Spot the dalmation on the trail of a thief . . . plus other favourite characters in seven exciting new stories!

HOME FARM TWINS
Jenny Oldfield

66127 5	Speckle The Stray	£3.99	❏
66128 3	Sinbad The Runaway	£3.99	❏
66129 1	Solo The Homeless	£3.99	❏
66130 5	Susie The Orphan	£3.99	❏
66131 3	Spike The Tramp	£3.99	❏
66132 1	Snip and Snap The Truants	£3.99	❏
68990 0	Sunny The Hero	£3.99	❏
68991 9	Socks The Survivor	£3.99	❏
68992 7	Stevie The Rebel	£3.99	❏
68993 5	Samson The Giant	£3.99	❏
69983 3	Sultan The Patient	£3.99	❏
69984 1	Sorrel The Substitute	£3.99	❏
69985 X	Skye The Champion	£3.99	❏
69986 8	Sugar and Spice The Pickpockets	£3.99	❏
69987 6	Sophie The Show-off	£3.99	❏
72682 2	Smoky The Mystery	£3.99	❏
72795 0	Scott The Braveheart	£3.99	❏
72796 9	Spot The Prisoner	£3.99	❏
727977	Shelley The Shadow	£3.99	❏

All Hodder Children's books are available at your local bookshop, or can be ordered direct from the publisher. Just tick the titles you would like and complete the details below. Prices and availability are subject to change without prior notice.

Please enclose a cheque or postal order made payable to *Bookpoint Ltd*, and send to: Hodder Children's Books, 39 Milton Park, Abingdon, OXON OX14 4TD, UK. Email Address: orders@bookpoint.co.uk

If you would prefer to pay by credit card, our call centre team would be delighted to take your order by telephone. Our direct line *01235 400414* (lines open 9.00 am–6.00 pm Monday to Saturday, 24 hour message answering service). Alternatively you can send a fax on *01235 400454*.

TITLE		FIRST NAME		SURNAME	

ADDRESS	
DAYTIME TEL:		POST CODE	

If you would prefer to pay by credit card, please complete:
Please debit my Visa/Access/Diner's Card/American Express (delete as applicable) card no:

				·														

Signature .... Expiry Date: ....

If you would NOT like to receive further information on our products please tick the box. ❏